WITHDRAWN

Squabbling Squashes

Carol Lingman and **Shohaku Okumura**
Illustrated by **Minette Mangahas**

Waterford Township Public Library
5168 Civic Center Drive
Waterford MI 48329
248-674-4831

In the country of Japan,
there are many Buddhist temples.

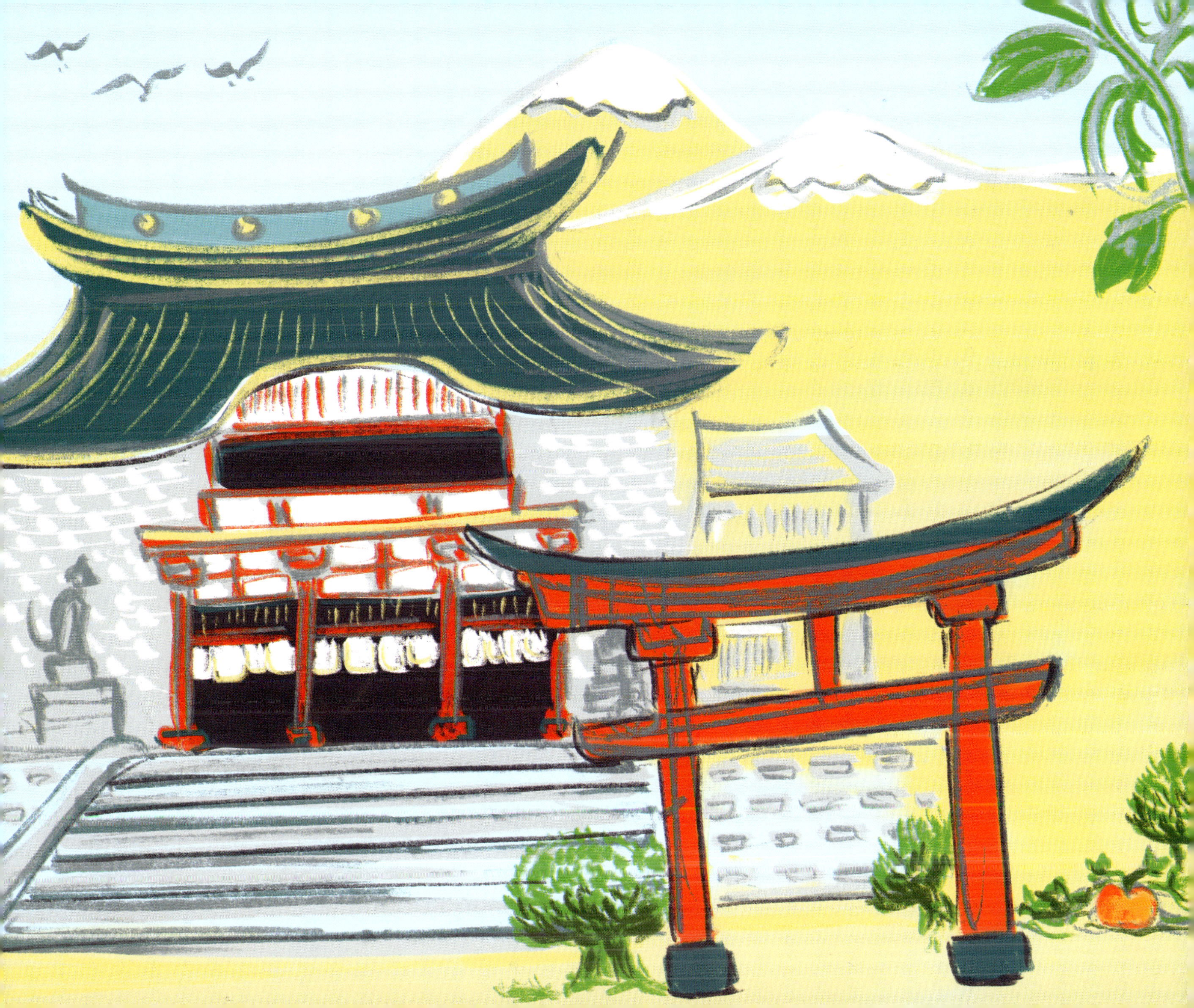

Some of the Buddhist temples are in cities and are very big, with lots of monks living there.

And some are very small with only a few monks.

One of the temples in the
country has a big garden behind it.
It is the temple where Monk Joshin lives.

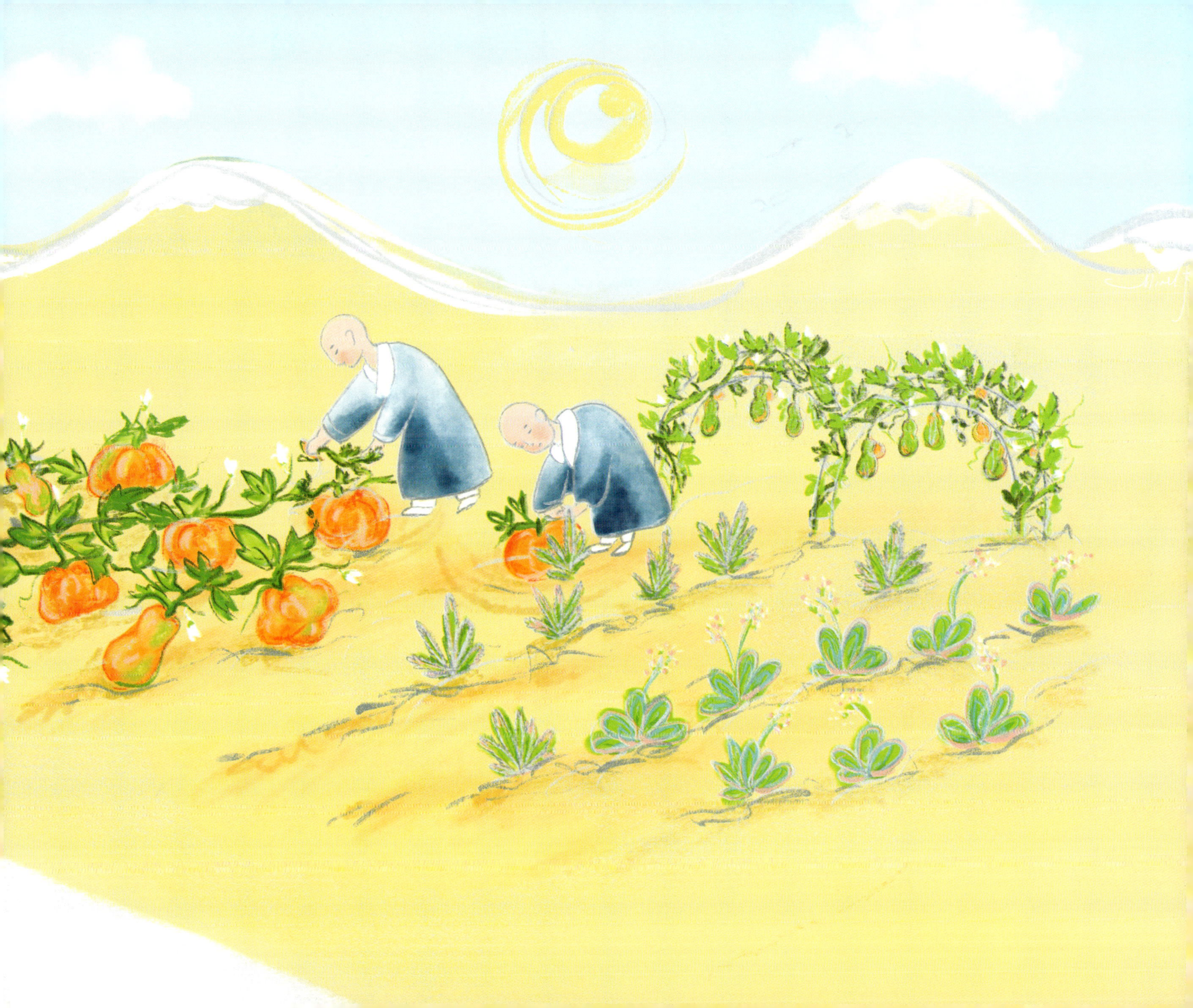

Monk Joshin and all the monks
who live in the temple grow vegetables
in the garden to make delicious meals.

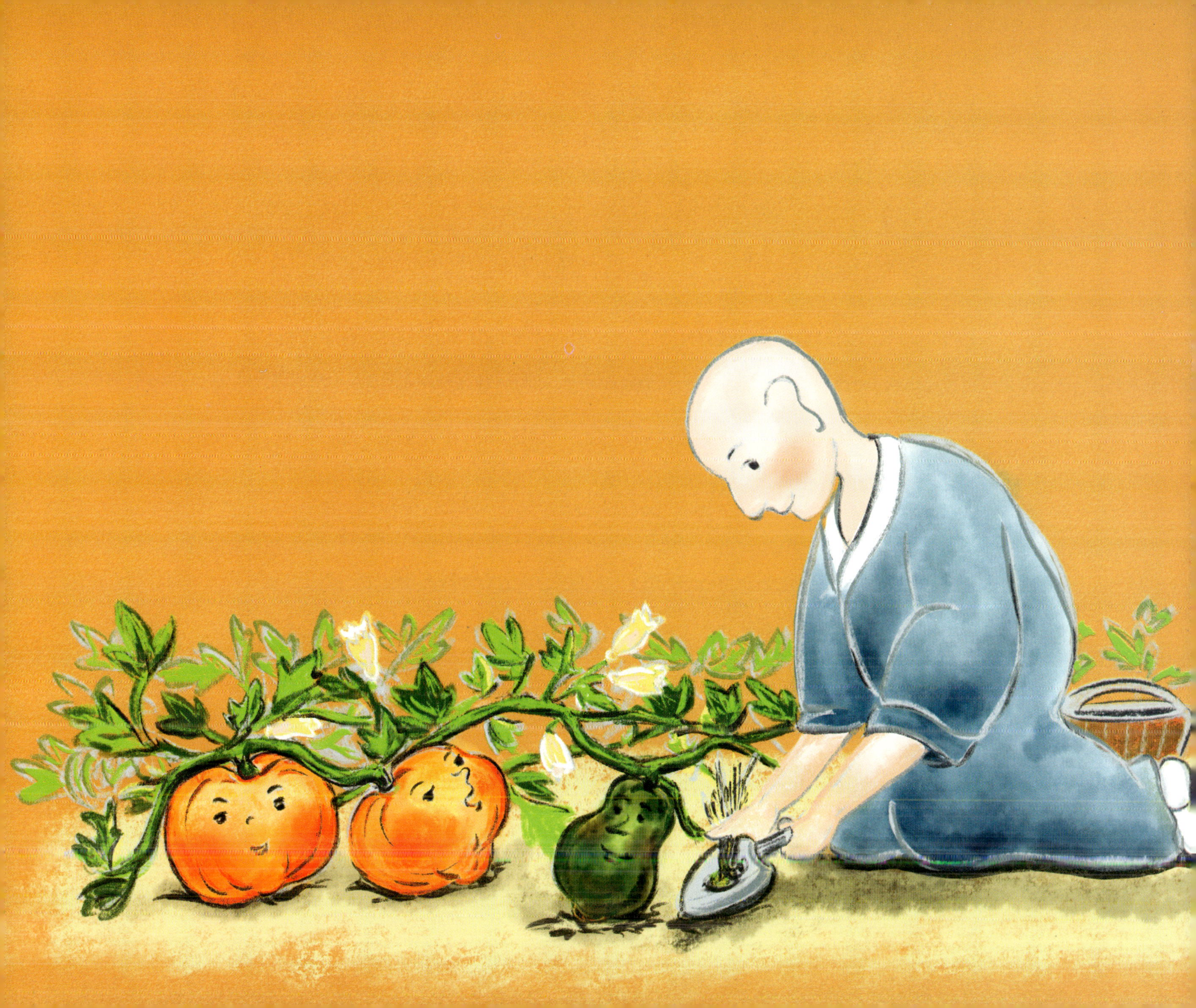

One of Monk Joshin's favorite vegetables is squash.
There are many squashes growing in a
long line in the garden. The squashes are very
happy in the garden because the monks take
very good care of them . . . giving them water . . .
and using small hoes to take away the weeds.
So they grow to be very healthy squashes.

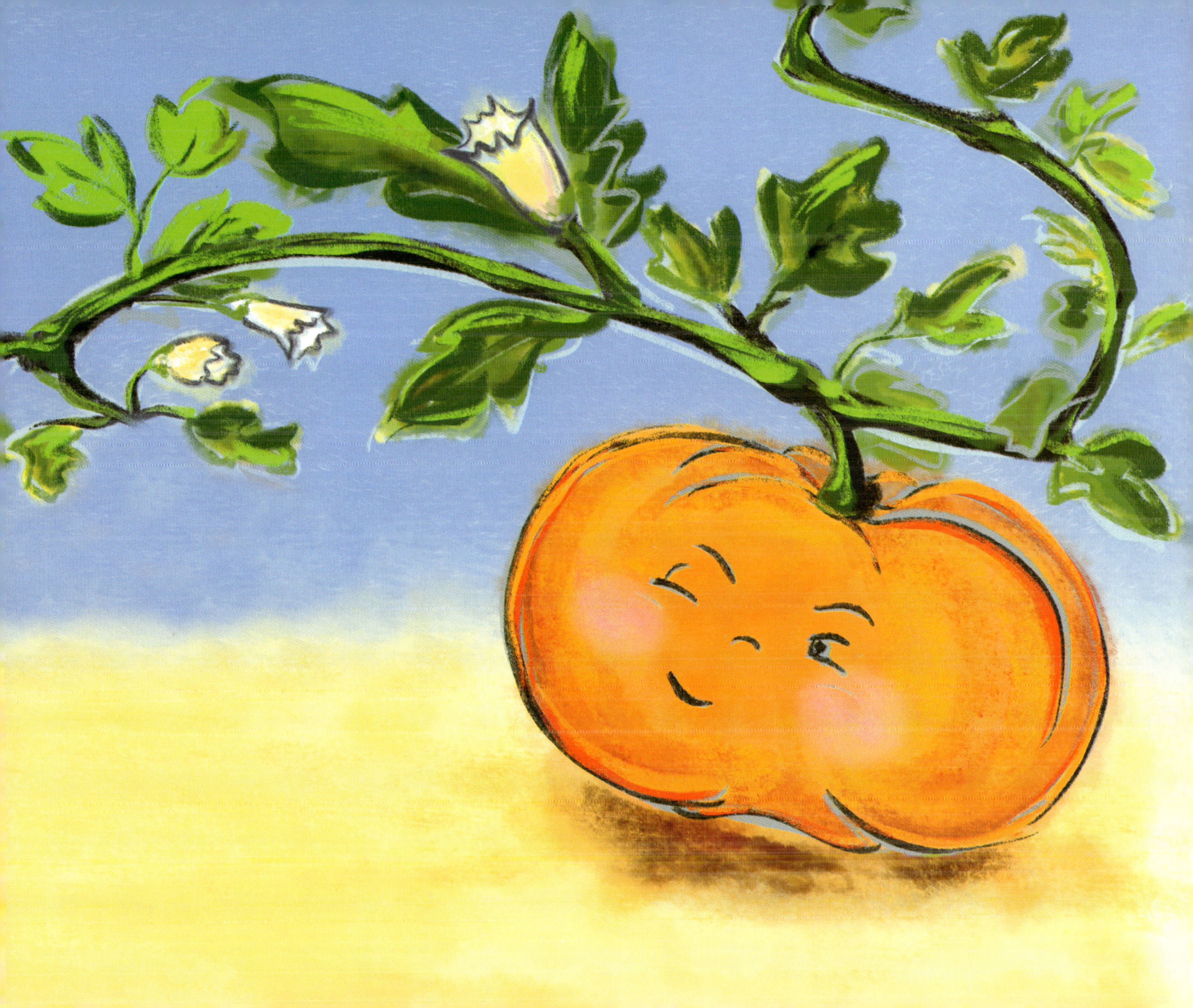

One day, the monks hear a lot of noise coming from the garden.

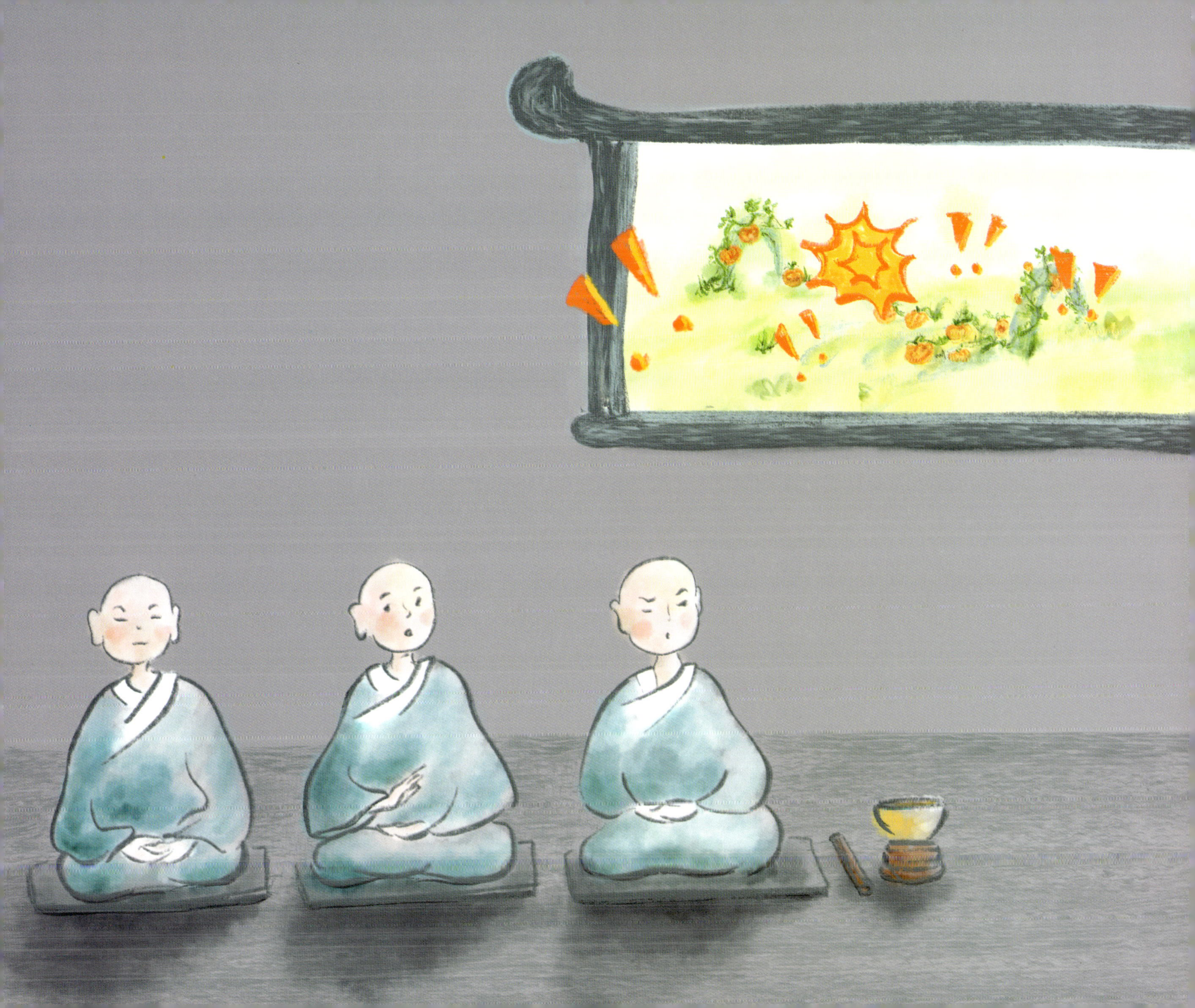

The squashes are shouting at each other. They are fighting about who is the most beautiful squash . . . and who is the squash that the monks like the most.

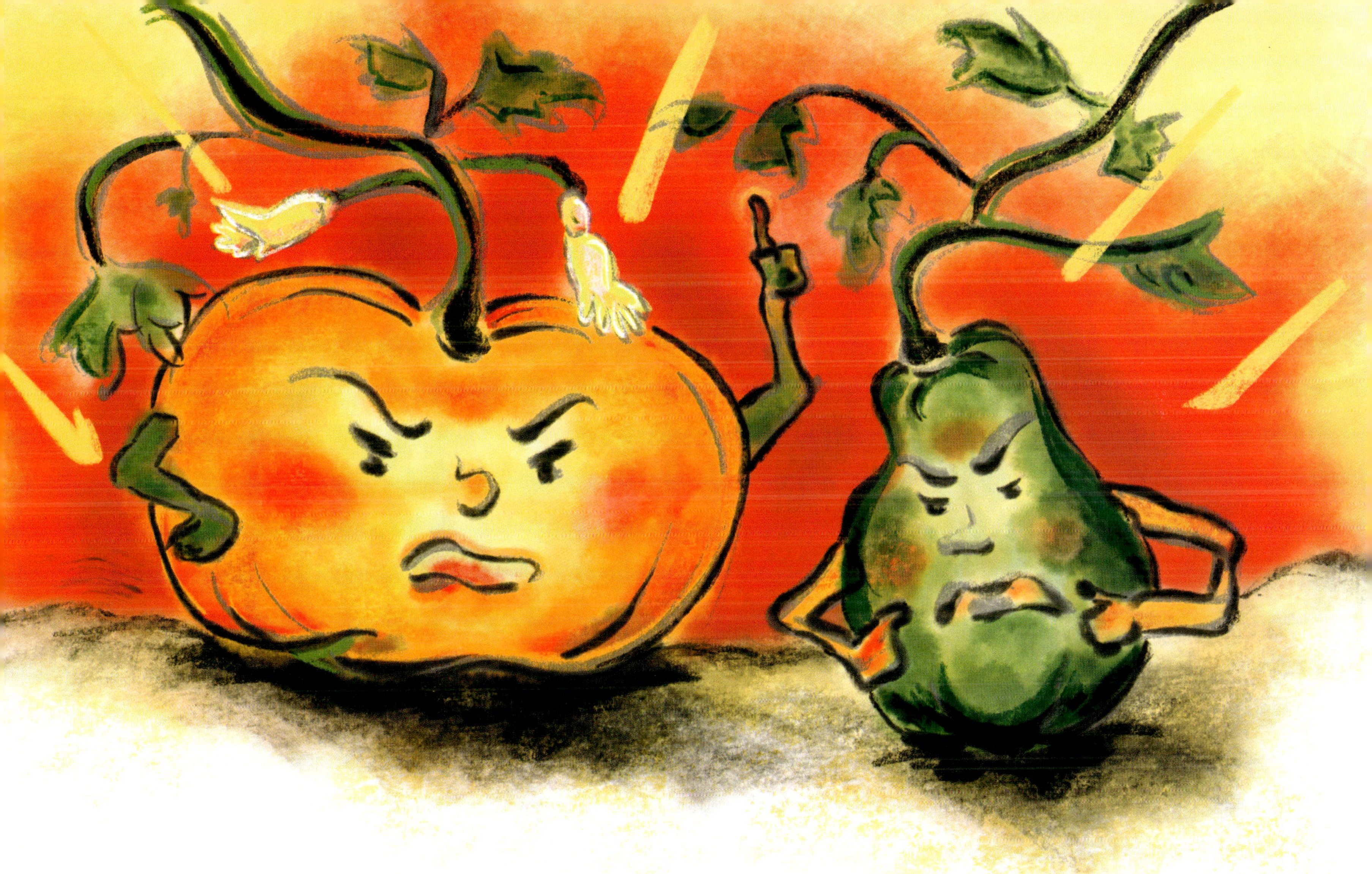

Monk Joshin comes into the garden
to see what all the fuss is about.
He says in a loud voice, "Hey, you squashes.
You seem to be getting very upset.
Let me teach you something that might help."

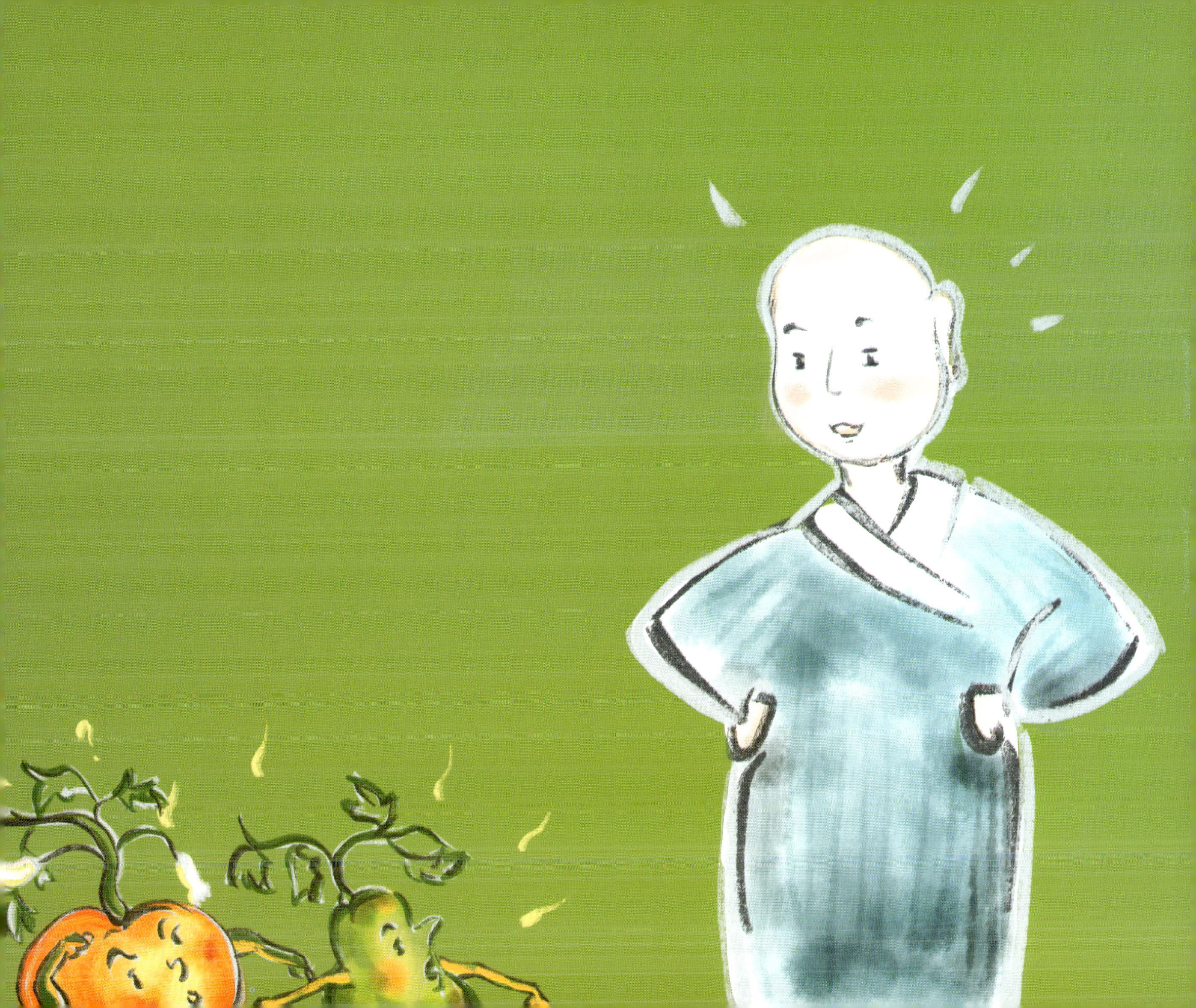

Then he shows them how to become quiet.
He says, "Try this: Sit up nice and straight.
And hold your hands like this. Lower your eyes,
and try not to look around. There is no need to
say anything. Just sit quietly, breathing in and out."

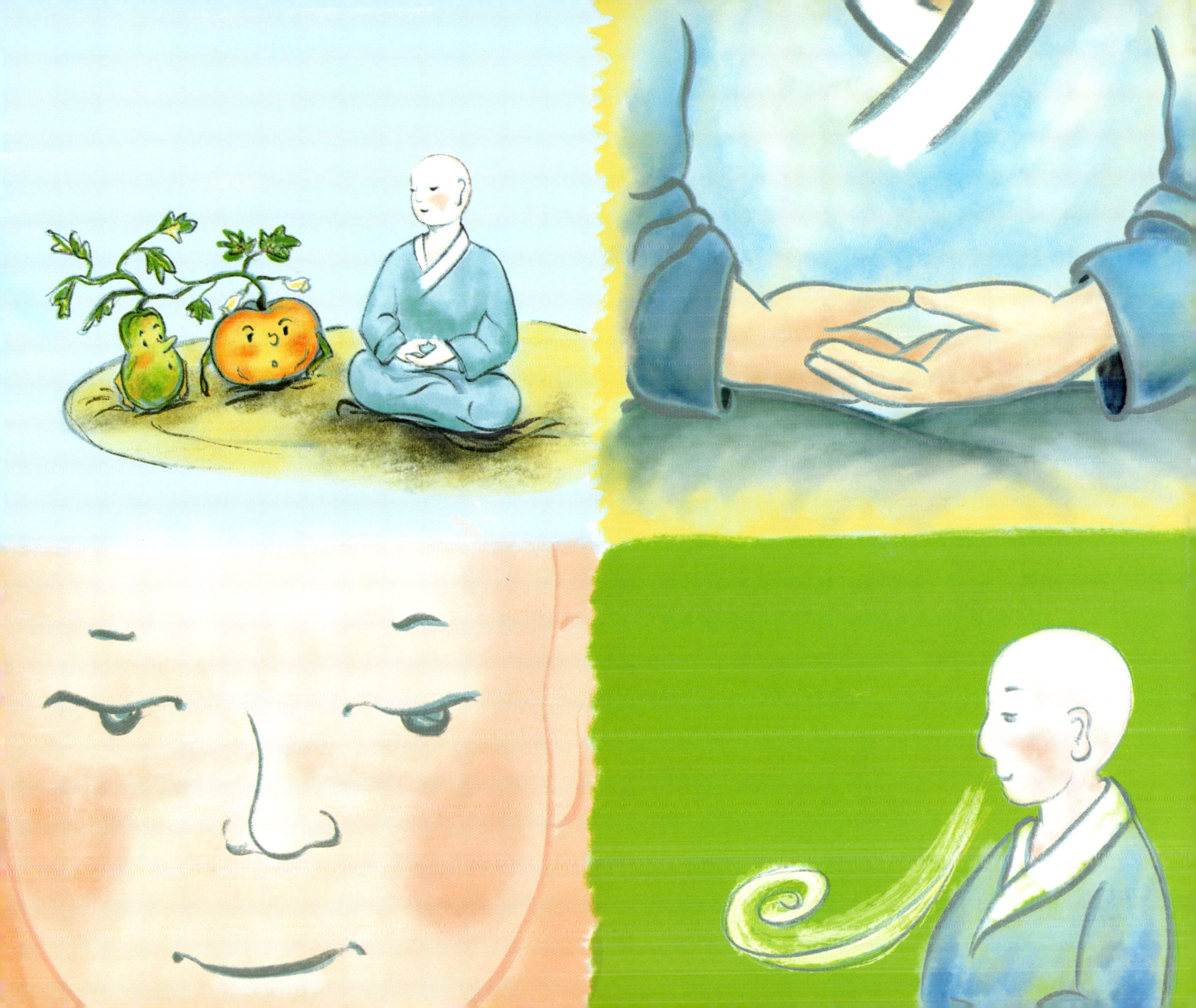

The squashes begin to sit like Monk Joshin
shows them . . . and they become less angry . . .
and they stop yelling and squabbling.
They become more and more quiet . . . and peaceful.

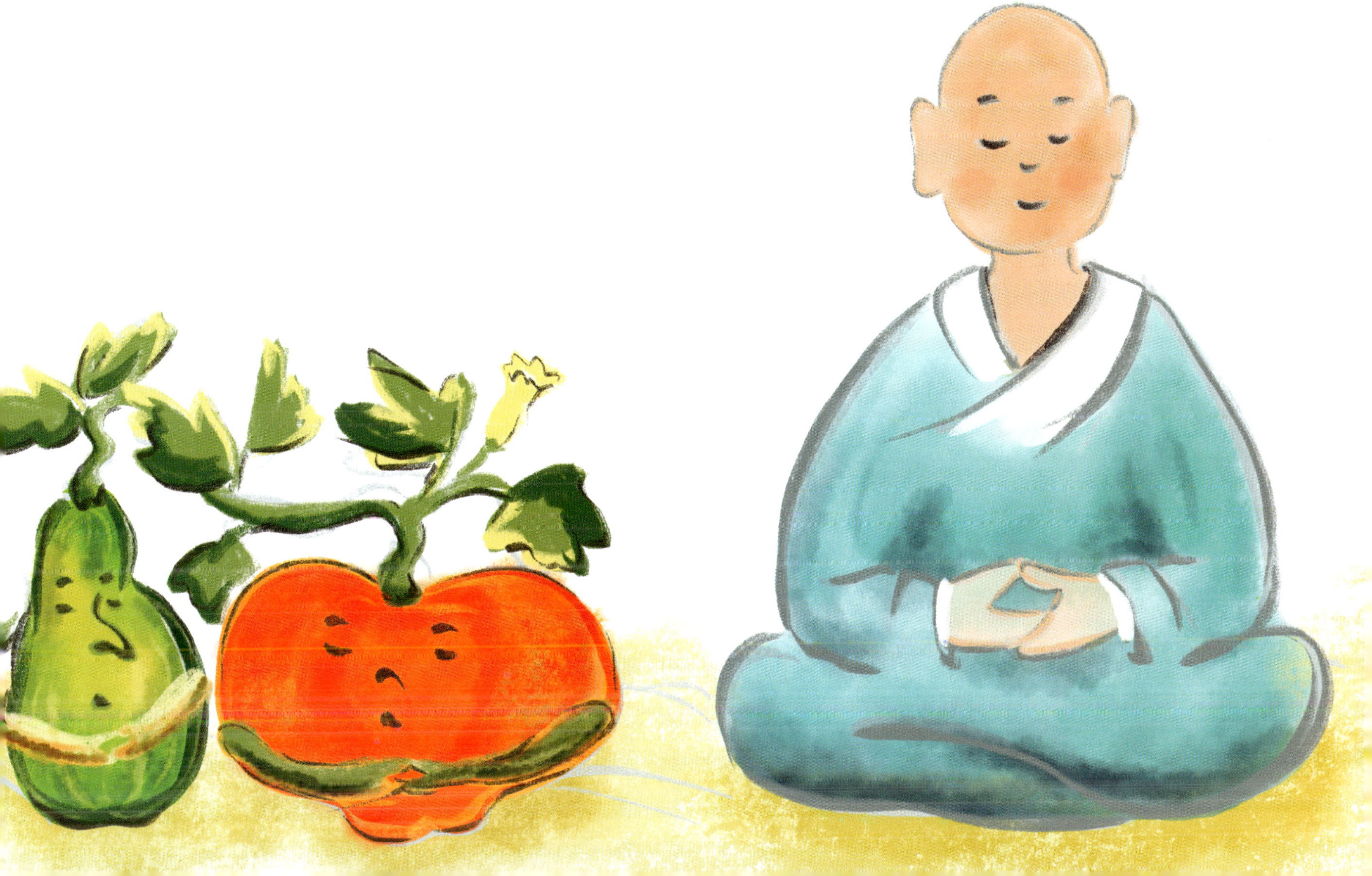

Then Monk Joshin says in a very quiet voice, "Now, squashes, put your hands on top of your heads."

The squashes put their hands on the tops of their heads. And when they do, one of them says, "This is very strange. There is something attached to the top of my head."

They see there is a *vine* that connects all of them together.

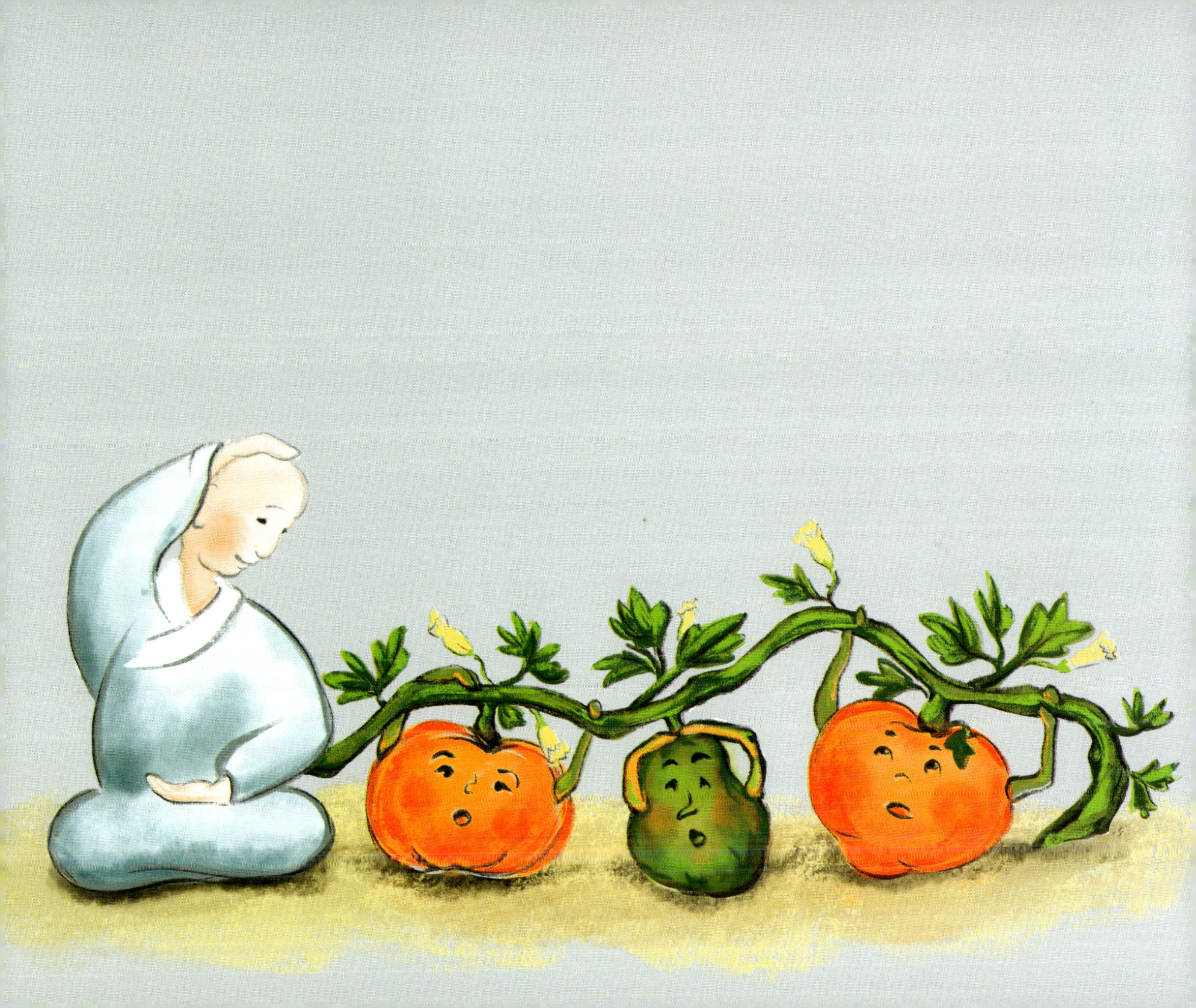

One of the squashes says, "Hey, squashes! We are all tied together. We are all on the same vine."

Monk Joshin nods his head.
"Yes, you are all connected. You live together on the same vine."

The squashes think about this. Then one of them says, "It's true that we are all different squashes . . . some are bigger and some are smaller . . . some are rounder and some are longer. But even if we are different, we are all connected. We are all growing together.

We don't have to be squabbling squashes.

We can live together in the monks' garden in peaceful connection."

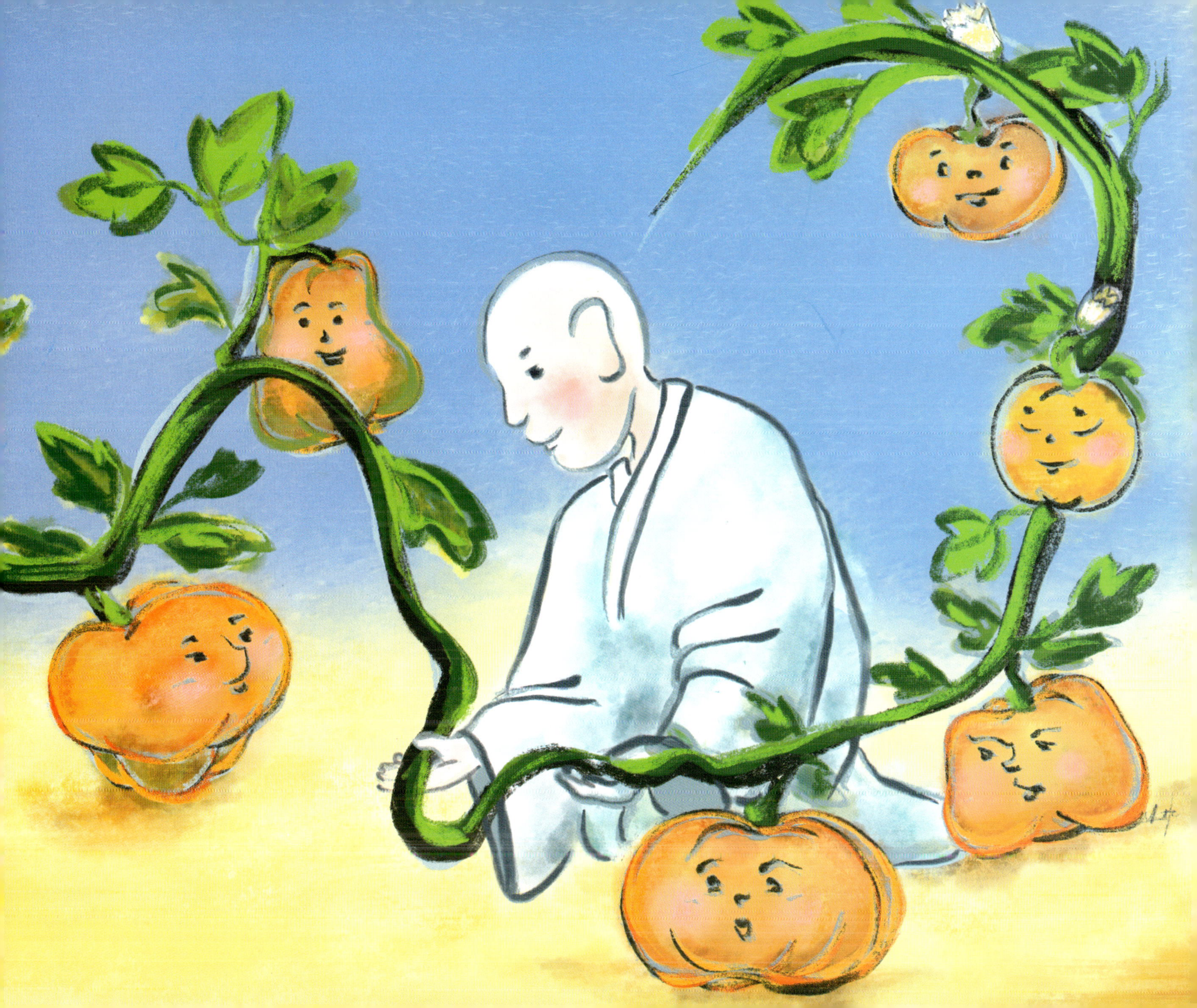

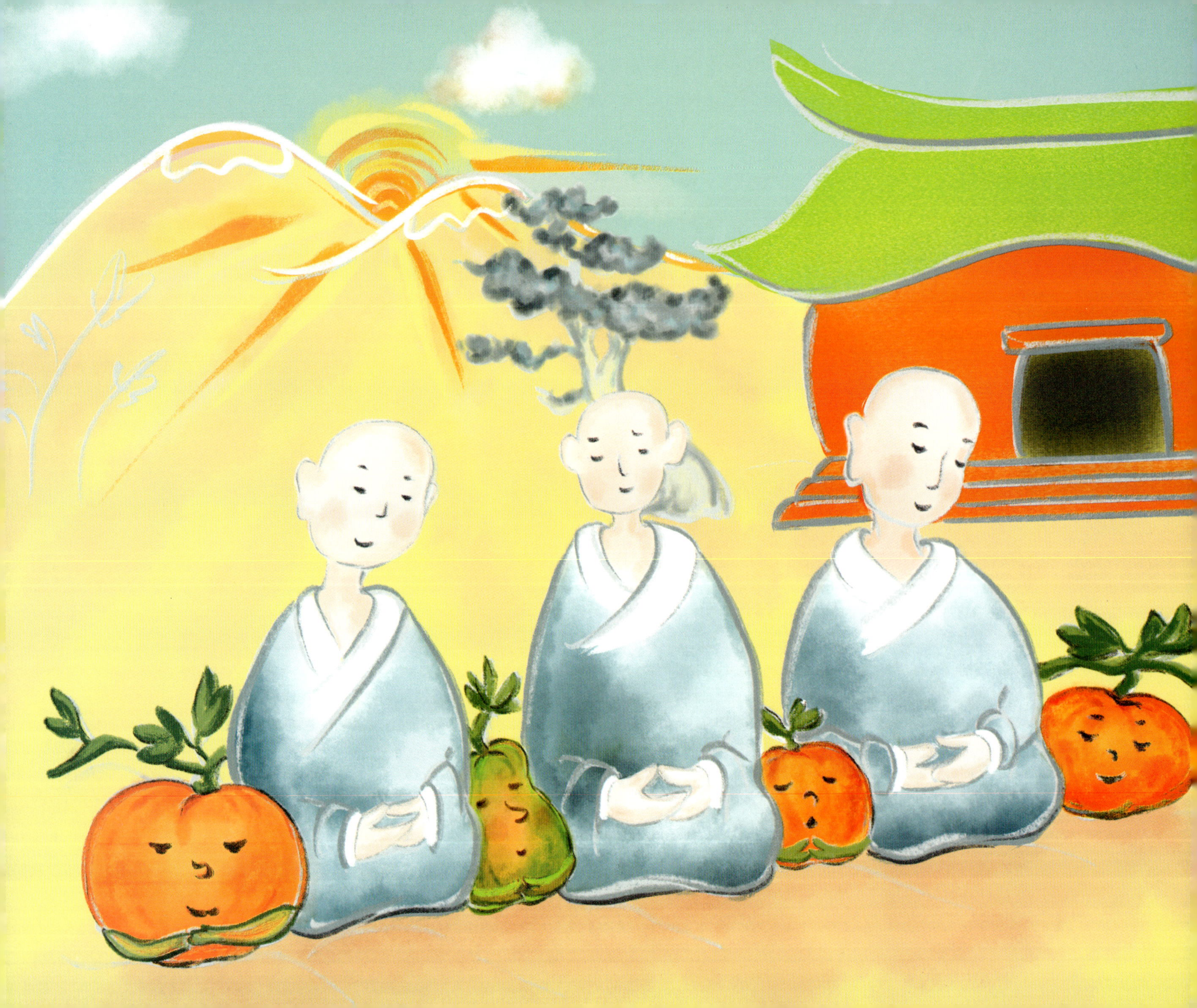

And so they did.

AFTERWORD

My teacher, Kosho Uchiyama Roshi, introduced this story of squabbling squashes in his book *Opening the Hand of Thought*. The original source is unknown, though Uchiyama Roshi said that it is a story from the Edo period (1603–1868) in Japan, but he did not say where he found it. Uchiyama Roshi's Dharma brother, Kozan Yoshida Roshi, also mentioned a different version of a similar story in his book. So it seems that this story was known among the disciples of Kodo Sawaki Roshi, a famous Zen master of the early twentieth century.

One of the most important teachings in Mahayana Buddhism is the truth of "interdependent origination." As a symbol of interconnectedness, Indra's Net from the Avatamsaka Sutra (Flower Ornament Sutra) is often used, a vast net throughout the entire universe in which every knot or node has a jewel reflecting every other jewel in the net. This story of squabbling squashes is a Japanese Zen version of Indra's net. I think it is a more concrete and visible image of our way of being in relation with all other beings. When we sit and become more calm, we begin to see that we are living together with all other beings in nature on the planet Earth, the same as the squashes discovering that they are all connected and living One Life through the vines.

I want to express my appreciation to Carol Lingman and to the illustrator, Minette Mangahas, for their excellent work to make this a story that children can enjoy, and through it, understand the preciousness of our lives connected with all beings.

—Shohaku Okumura

ABOUT THE AUTHORS AND ILLUSTRATOR

Shohaku Okumura is the abbot of Sanshin Zen Community in Bloomington, Indiana. He is the author of many books on Zen Buddhism and continues to lead intensive meditation retreats at Sanshin-ji and other centers in the United States and around the world.

Carol Lingman is a Zen practitioner and retired editor living in Sonoma County, California where she practices East Asian calligraphy and the Feldenkrais Method. She has written and edited many educational, environmental, and movement studies publications for adults. This is her first children's book.

Minette Mangahas is an artist and designer whose calligraphy-inspired work has been featured internationally. When not illustrating squashes, she's eating them.

AFTERWORD

My teacher, Kosho Uchiyama Roshi, introduced this story of squabbling squashes in his book *Opening the Hand of Thought.* The original source is unknown, though Uchiyama Roshi said that it is a story from the Edo period (1603–1868) in Japan, but he did not say where he found it. Uchiyama Roshi's Dharma brother, Kozan Yoshida Roshi, also mentioned a different version of a similar story in his book. So it seems that this story was known among the disciples of Kodo Sawaki Roshi, a famous Zen master of the early twentieth century.

One of the most important teachings in Mahayana Buddhism is the truth of "interdependent origination." As a symbol of interconnectedness, Indra's Net from the Avatamsaka Sutra (Flower Ornament Sutra) is often used, a vast net throughout the entire universe in which every knot or node has a jewel reflecting every other jewel in the net. This story of squabbling squashes is a Japanese Zen version of Indra's net. I think it is a more concrete and visible image of our way of being in relation with all other beings. When we sit and become more calm, we begin to see that we are living together with all other beings in nature on the planet Earth, the same as the squashes discovering that they are all connected and living One Life through the vines.

I want to express my appreciation to Carol Lingman and to the illustrator, Minette Mangahas, for their excellent work to make this a story that children can enjoy, and through it, understand the preciousness of our lives connected with all beings.

—Shohaku Okumura

ABOUT THE AUTHORS AND ILLUSTRATOR

Shohaku Okumura is the abbot of Sanshin Zen Community in Bloomington, Indiana. He is the author of many books on Zen Buddhism and continues to lead intensive meditation retreats at Sanshin-ji and other centers in the United States and around the world.

Carol Lingman is a Zen practitioner and retired editor living in Sonoma County, California where she practices East Asian calligraphy and the Feldenkrais Method. She has written and edited many educational, environmental, and movement studies publications for adults. This is her first children's book.

Minette Mangahas is an artist and designer whose calligraphy-inspired work has been featured internationally. When not illustrating squashes, she's eating them.

Wisdom Publications
199 Elm Street
Somerville, MA 02144 USA
wisdomexperience.org

Text © 2021 Carol Lingman
Illustrations © 2021 Minette Mangahas
All rights reserved.

No part of this book may be reproduced in any form or by any means, electronic or mechanical, including photography, recording, or by any information storage and retrieval system or technologies now known or later developed, without permission in writing from the publisher.

Designed by Katrina Damkoehler.

Printed on acid-free paper that meets the guidelines for permanence and durability of the Production Guidelines for Book Longevity of the Council on Library Resources.

Printed in Malaysia.

Library of Congress Cataloging-in-Publication Data
Names: Lingman, Carol, author. | Okumura, Shohaku, 1948– author. | Mangahas, Minette, illustrator.
Title: Squabbling squashes / Carol Lingman and Shohaku Okumura; illustrator, Minette Mangahas.
Description: Somerville, MA: Wisdom Publications, [2021] | Audience: Grades 2–3
Identifiers: LCCN 2020040367 (print) | LCCN 2020040368 (ebook) | ISBN 9781614296935 (hardcover) | ISBN 9781614296928 (ebook)
Subjects: LCSH: Buddhist legends—Japan—Juvenile literature. | Harmony (Philosophy)—Religious aspects—Buddhism—Juvenile literature.
Classification: LCC BQ5815 .L56 2021 (print) | LCC BQ5815 (ebook) | DDC 294.3/444—dc23
LC record available at https://lccn.loc.gov/2020040367
LC ebook record available at https://lccn.loc.gov/2020040368

ISBN 978-1-61429-693-5
ebook ISBN 978-1-61429-692-8

25 24 23 22 21   5 4 3 2 1

About Wisdom Publications

Wisdom Publications is the leading publisher of classic and contemporary Buddhist books and practical works on mindfulness. To learn more about us or to explore our other books, please visit our website at wisdomexperience.org or contact us at the address below.

Wisdom Publications
199 Elm Street
Somerville, MA 02144 USA

We are a 501(c)(3) organization, and donations in support of our mission are tax deductible.

Wisdom Publications is affiliated with the Foundation for the Preservation of the Mahayana Tradition (FPMT).

Waterford Township Public Library
5168 Civic Center Drive
Waterford MI 48329
248-674-4831